To the children of Afghanistan

The Circus Comes to the Village

Yutaka Kobayashi

Museyon, New York

Autumn has come.

The long-awaited circus has come to the village
of Paghman in the mountains of Afghanistan.

Yamo comes home from school as fast as his legs can carry him.

His friend Mirado follows, playing his flute.

♫ BOOM! BOOM! RAT-A-TAT! PAP-PAP-PAP ♫
The drums and trumpets of the traveling circus are heard in the fields below.

"Mom, the circus has come! It's the circus!!"

Yamo's mother is kneading naan bread with Mirado's grandmother. She looks up and smiles at Yamo, but says, "Your work in the fields is waiting, you know. Work extra hard today and you can go tomorrow." Mirado's grandmother agrees. Reluctantly Yamo and Mirado walk to the fields.

There is so much to be done in the fields.
Yamo and Mirado join everyone to gather wheat and yams.

Because they did not have much snow last winter, there are fewer crops this year. "But it looks like we've got enough to make it through the winter," says Yamo's father hopefully.

Finally they finish their work. "Let's go see the circus together tomorrow. Okay, Mirado?" "Sure!" Mirado goes home by the mountain pass as he plays his flute.

The muffled boom of a cannon comes from afar. Mirado's father went to the war and hasn't returned yet. Mirado is always playing the flute that his father left behind. The melody floats into the far mountains.

That night, the villagers can hear the
circus people working in the village
square until late, setting up the tent
and assembling large pieces of wood.
"What on earth are they building?"
Yamo is excited by the sounds,
but he finally falls asleep.

In the morning, the village square is crowded with villagers.
A large tent has been set up. There's even a Ferris wheel and
spinning swing ride!
The man at the Ferris wheel calls out,
"Come over here. You'll see the world!"
Many stalls are lined up, selling toys, food, and all kinds of things.

There is sweet rice pudding
and parched barley cookies,
honey and chocolate.

The toy shop has toy trains and
pinwheels, yo-yos and kites.
Everything is here!

Ice cream is only
for watching.

"Hi, Bird-shop man, how much is
this bird?"
"Hey, boy, why don't you buy it?"
"........."

Yamo and Mirado ride on the spinning swing.

They fly around so fast it's as if they were birds themselves!

The square and the village go round and round.

The boys go so fast that they are dizzy when they

get off the ride. No one can walk straight.

BOOM, BOOM, BA-BOOM!!
That's the sound of a big drum.
A man calls out,
"This is the most fun circus in the world!
See the mysterious iron man and the scary fire-eating man!
We've got worlds full of wonder.
Come on, everybody, the show starts now!
You pay on your way out after watching!"
The villagers start gathering around.
Yamo's heart is pounding.

He groans—"Uhh . . ."—and lifts up seven children at the same time!

The mysterious iron man has huge, muscular arms.

The fire-eating man blows fire from his mouth.

But, being overly enthusiastic, he singes his hair and beard!

Everyone roars with laughter.

Then a beautiful woman walks onstage, singing. For the first time, Yamo sees a lady who is even more beautiful than his mom.

♫ Shiranui, my love,
Where have you gone?
Gone to a war in a faraway land.
Shiranui, my love,
Searching for you,
I travel to Bukhara from Samarkand ♫

Everyone is enchanted by her lovely voice. As she sings,
Mirado begins playing his flute.
Everyone listens silently to the sweet harmony.
"Well, little artist, come on up here." The singer invites Mirado up onto the stage.

Together with the band, Mirado plays songs that capture everyone's hearts.

"Bravo, Mirado!!"
The delighted audience stands up, applauding.

"Encore! Mirado!!"

"That was so much fun, wasn't it?" "Our village is the best in the world!"

How I wish every day were like this, Yamo thought.

The next morning, there is no more Ferris wheel or swing ride in the village square. The tent has shrunk and looks awkward. The fun circus is over.

Mirado tells Yamo excitedly,
    "The circus people loved my music. My grandma says I can go with the circus!"

Mirado is leaving.

"Mirado is so lucky. He is going to have fun every day. Right, Dad?"

Yamo's father just smiles.

Yamo and Mirado hug one another. Then they exchange a farewell greeting like the adults do, by touching cheek to cheek.

"Good-bye, Mirado. While you travel, you should be able to see your dad, too."

Once the circus leaves, the villagers get busy preparing for the harsh winter.
The sky turns dull and cloudy, and a cold wind starts to blow.

As the wind blows Yamo thinks,

"I wonder how Mirado is doing. Did he get to see his dad?"

Then, one day, snow comes to the village.

"It's snowing! The first snow!" Everyone has been waiting for this because snow promises good crops next year.

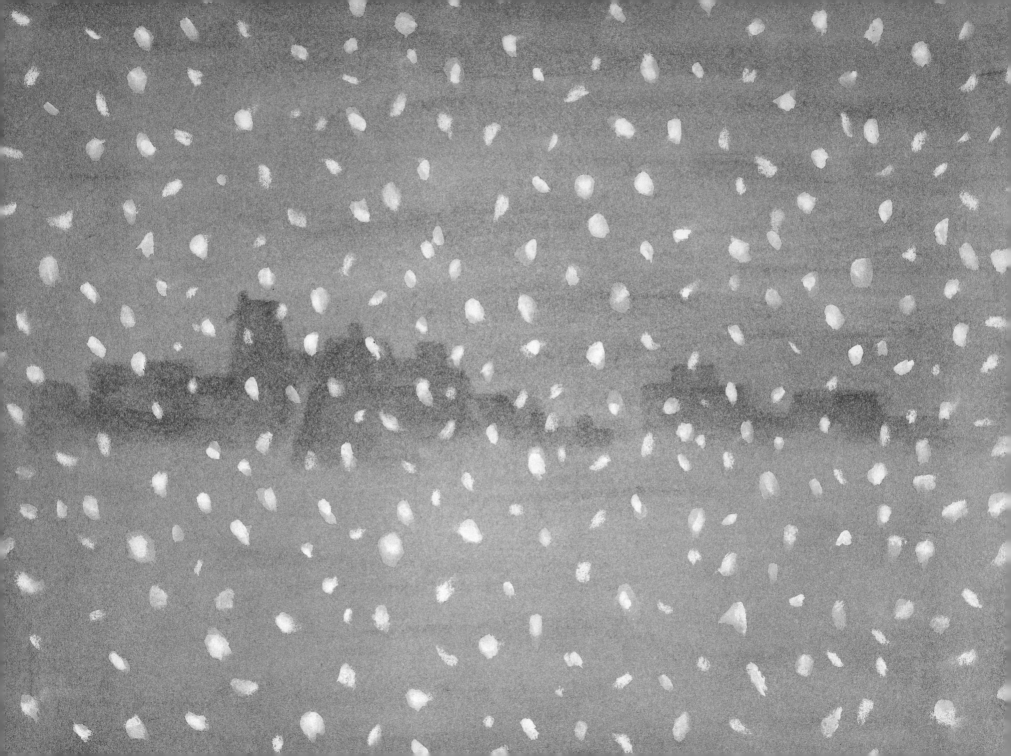

But that winter, the village was destroyed in the war. The people barely escaped with their lives and moved to other places.

Now no one lives in the village.

However, as spring always follows a harsh winter, the village of Paghman waits quietly for everyone's return.

The Circus Comes to the Village

Boku no Mura ni Circus ga kita © 1996 Yutaka Kobayashi
All rights reserved.

Published in the United States / Canada by:
Museyon Inc.
333 East 45th Street
New York, NY 10017

Museyon is a registered trademark.
Visit us online at www.museyon.com

Originally published in Japan in 1996 by POPLAR Publishing Co., Ltd.
English translation rights arranged with POPLAR Publishing Co., Ltd.

Printed in China

ISBN 978-1-940842-27-1